FROM THE FILMS OF

Harry Potter™

GLOW-IN-THE-DARK
COLORING BOOK

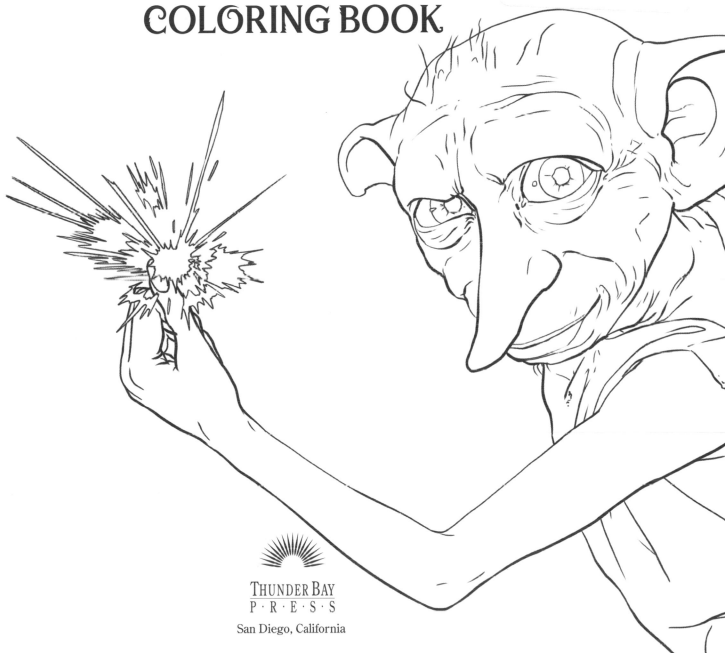

THUNDER BAY
P·R·E·S·S

San Diego, California

Thunder Bay Press
An imprint of Printers Row Publishing Group
9717 Pacific Heights Blvd, San Diego, CA 92121
www.thunderbaybooks.com • mail@thunderbaybooks.com

Printers Row Publishing Group is a division of Readerlink Distribution Services, LLC.
Thunder Bay Press is a registered trademark of Readerlink Distribution Services, LLC.

Correspondence regarding the content of this book should be sent to Thunder Bay Press, Editorial
Department, at the above address.

Thunder Bay Press
Publisher: Peter Norton
Associate Publisher: Ana Parker
Art Director: Charles McStravick
Senior Developmental Editor: Diane Cain
Editor: Jessica Matteson
Production Team: Beno Chan, Rusty von Dyl, Mimi Oey

Format Development, Design & Special Effects produced by Red Bird Publishing UK.

ISBN: 978-1-64517-900-9

Printed, manufactured, and assembled in Heshan, China.

26 25 24 23 22   2 3 4 5 6

THE WIZARDING WORLD is an incredible place filled with beloved characters, beautiful locations, and fantastic creatures. This intricately drawn coloring book allows you to fill in every magical detail—from the shades of pink in Dolores Umbridge's uniquely decorated office to the bright red-and-yellow plumage of Fawkes the phoenix.

Color your way through Harry Potter's seven years at Hogwarts School of Witchcraft and Wizardry, as he sees Hogwarts castle for the first time, soars across the Quidditch pitch, competes in the Triwizard Tournament, and forms lifelong friendships with Ron Weasley, Hermione Granger, Luna Lovegood, Neville Longbottom, and Ginny Weasley.

Twenty glow-in-the-dark pages reveal the flicker of Headmaster Albus Dumbledore's Deluminator, the glint of gold at Gringotts, the flame of the Goblet of Fire, the majesty of Hogwarts castle, and more when you turn off the lights.

No wand, spell, or potion is needed to experience the magic of the Wizarding World in this book! Simply use your favorite colored pencils or markers to bring each incredible scene to life. Then, make the room dark to see your masterpiece glow! Each page is perforated, so you can easily tear out your creations to frame, display, or trade with friends.

Relive the best moments from the Harry Potter films with *Harry Potter Glow-in-the-Dark Coloring Book!*

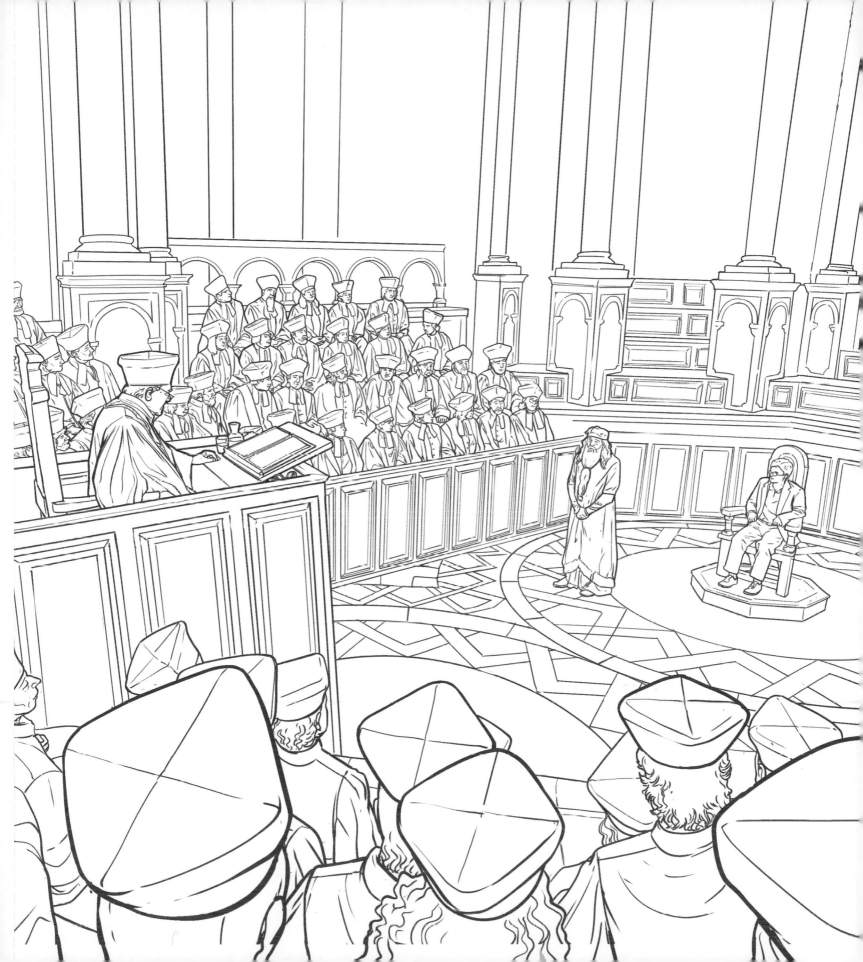